Royal and Her Brother King

Joslynn Dixon

Royal Media & Publishing
Jeffersonville, IN 47131
http://www.royalmediaandpublishing.com
royalmediapublishing@gmail.com

ISBN: 978-1-955501-38-5

Printed in the United States of America

Dedication

I dedicate this book to every sister and brother who has a very special bond with each other, that nobody can t never break apart no matter what.

Acknowledgements

I like to think the big man upstairs who helps me come up with the ideas, who pushed me to do something different and the strength to keep writing when I thought it was taking too long and felt like giving up. I had self-doubt because I kept feeling like this book is not going to go no where like my last two books, but He has me keeping the faith.

Table of Contents

Dedication iii

Acknowledgements v

Introduction viii

Chapter One 1

Chapter Two 11

Chapter Three 17

Chapter Four 21

Chapter Five 33

Chapter Six 39

Chapter Seven 47

About the Author 59

More Books By This Author 60

Introduction

I have seen how different and special the bond is between boy and girl siblings. It's amazing to me watching the people around me who have a brother or a sister and how they reach out to each other. It is amazing how much love they have for each other has had me wanting to write something that siblings that can relate to and celebrate each other.

Contact Information:

Email the author – franklingril@yahoo.com

Facebook – Joslynn.Dixon

Email the publisher at: royalmediaandpublishing@gmail.com

Chapter One

Royal is an eighteen-year-old, smart, loving, caring, beautiful, sweet-hearted girl who has a very big heart. She also has dreams and goals of being an herbal medical doctor. Royal graduated with a 4.30 grade average. She was the top of her class. She got accepted to thirty colleges, including UCT Health Science Center, which is her dream college, the one she has always wanted to go for her medical degree. She says it's the best school for what she wants to study. She works at Footlocker, so she can save for a car and for college. Royal stays at home with her parents and with her brother, King, who is her best friend. They are from San Diego and the siblings are close. Their parents raised them to be that way. They also taught them their culture and that family is everything, no matter what. So, King and Royal take that to heart.

King is a nineteen-year-old, smart, funny, sweet, respectful, caring boy. He graduated with a 4.60, at the top of his class as well. He works at an unassisted contract company. His dreams and goals are to save his money, so he can own his own unassisted contract company, in his own city.

"Damn," King yelled out with anger.

"What?" Royal asked with panic in her voice as she ran to King's room.

"I just got robbed at gunpoint," King said as he sat down on his bed.

"Wait, what you mean you got robbed at gunpoint?" Royal asked.

"You heard me," King said.

"Oh my God, do you know who did it?" Royal asked.

"Yes, I do; it was James," King told her.

"Who is James?" Royal asked.

"James, the negro who be hanging around the block with his homies," King told Royal. "His homies are so stupid. They be sitting under him like he God or something. But only if they knew that James don't care nothing about them. They just there so he can make them do what he wants them to do and they dumb enough to do it."

"But how do you know it was him?" Royal asked.

"Because I know what car he's always in," King said.

"So, what are you going to do?" Royal asked.

"You already know what I'm going to do, sis," King told Royal.

"Okay, well, I'm going with you," Royal replied.

"Okay, but one thing you have to do for me. You have to do what I say at all times. You understand, Royal?" King asked.

"Yes, I understand," Royal replied.

"King, how will we find him, because you don't chill with him, to know his whereabouts?" Royal asked.

"No, I don't be chilling with him like that. But I do know where he and his homies be all the time," King agreed.

"How will you know then?" Royal asked with an attitude.

"Well, big lips," King laughed and continued, "they be at James' house, across the tracks."

"Now, how do you know that?" Royal asked.

"Because I asked one of my homies where can I get some kush. He gave me this address to go to, so I went to it, and when I got there, I saw James standing outside, talking to my homie. So, when my homie got in the car, I asked him what James was doing there. He told me that was James' house. He's the only one with the kush. So, that's how I know," King said.

There was a loud *smack* then.

"Ayyyy, that hurt. Why you smack me like that?" King asked Royal while laughing.

"So, you smoking now? What's funny is I'm about to smack you again."

"Wait, wait," King said, chuckling again. "I don't smoke like that. I just smoke a little bit when work is stressing me. I was stressing that day."

"You know what, don't even worry about it. I can't with you. Anyways, what are we going to tell Mom and Dad for the reason why we leaving the house at 9pm?" Royal asked.

"We're just going to have to tell them the truth, just in case something bad happens and we need them," King replied.

"Okay," Royal said.

"So, when 9 o'clock gets here, we will go tell them before we leave," King said.

"Okay, but what if they don't let us go, then what?" Royal asked.

"Oh, they going to let us go, after I tell them he put a gun to my head. That's all I got to say, and they going to say, 'do what you got to do.'," King reasoned.

"Okay, we'll see," Royal said.

"So, until then, just be normal, and I will see you at 9," King told her while walking toward his room.

As time went by, King and Royal did what they normally did when they were at home.

9 o'clock finally came.

Knock, knock.

"Who is it?" Royal asked.

"It's King."

"Come in," Royal said.

"You ready?" he asked as he stood in the doorway dressed all in black.

"Yes, I am," Royal replied, with all black clothes on as well.

"Good, now, let's go tell Mom and

Dad what's up," King told Royal.

The brother and sister team walked to the living room where their parents were sitting.

"Mom, Dad, Royal and I have to tell y'all something," King began.

"I see that, son," their dad said.

"So, what's up, you two?" asked their mom.

"When I left the store to get in my car, I got robbed at gunpoint—"

"What? Wait, son, what you mean you got robbed at gunpoint?" King's mom asked, interrupting him.

"Do you know who did it?" their dad asked.

"Yes, I do," King told him. "It was James. That negro that be hanging around the block."

"Are you sure, baby?" his mom asked.

"Yes, I'm sure. I know the car he's always in."

"Well, son, you do what you have to do. Just be careful, and make sure you come back to us," King's dad told him.

"I will," King replied. "One more thing, y'all. Royal said she wants to come with me."

"The hell she is," King's mom yelled out.

"I told you she wasn't going to let me go with," Royal told her brother.

"So, you really want to go, baby girl?" her dad asked.

"Yes, I have to make sure he will be safe," Royal told her dad.

"Okay then," Dad said.

"Okay nothing. You heard what I said," Royal's mom said.

"No, let her go with him because, with her, he will come back safely," Royal's dad told their mom.

"What, are you serious? Royal and King?" Mom said to their dad. "Okay, if you believe that. Okay, I got y'all's backs," Mom finally agreed.

"But one thing, King," Dad added.

"Yes, Dad?" King asked.

"Make sure you keep your sister safe and both of y'all come home, you got me?"

"Yes, we got you," King and Royal said at the same time.

"You promise?" their dad asked.

"Yes," King told his dad. Turning to his sister, he said, "Let's go."

"Wait, King, since you are better at shooting long distance, I want you to take this 45 with the scope and silencer on it. And, Royal, since you just started to learn how to shoot, you take this 9mm," King and Royal's dad said. "And after whatever happens, y'all go to the safe house. Y'all do remember where the safe house is, don't you?

"Yes," King replied, "it's back in Los Angeles."

"Okay, good. When y'all get there,

turn your phones off, don’t call anybody, don’t use any type of electronic devices, and just wait for me until I get there. There's plenty of food there, so you won’t be hungry, and clean clothes are there to change into. Do not go outside or open the door for anybody. Y’all understand me?" their dad said to them.

"Yes, we understand," both King and Royal told their dad.

Chapter Two

Royal and King started walking out the front door.

"We love y'all, please be careful," King and Royal's mom said to them as they were walking out the door.

King and Royal got into King's car. King drove until they were a block away from James' house, then he parked his car behind an abandoned house.

"Come on; let's get out," he told Royal. They got out of the car.

"King, now I know this is not James' house," Royal said.

"Naw, crazy, his house is the next block over. I had to park here so no one would see my car or know who we are. We're going to have to walk to the next block from here. There is an abandoned house where we can wait and watch James' house. The house is across the street from James' house,"

King explained to Royal.

"Aw, man, I don’t want to walk," Royal said in a complaining voice.

"Don’t start that right now, Royal. We got to walk behind the houses so they won't see us," King told Royal.

"Ugh, okay," Royal said. King and Royal started walking. "What, why did you stop walking? Royal asked.

"This is the abandoned house," King told her. "I hope the back door isn't hard to get into, because I don’t want to break the window. I don’t want them to hear us." King tried to open the door. "Yes, it opened, so let’s go in before someone sees us, King told Royal.

King and Royal went into the abandoned house. "Look around, to see if you can find a good, dark spot with a good angle to see the house without being spotted," King suggested.

"Okay, got you," Royal said as she started walking.

King and Royal were walking around the house when Royal said, "King, King, I found a spot upstairs."

"Show me," King said.

"Okay, come on," Royal answered.

When King and Royal got to the room, he said, "Okay, yeah, this will do, but let's make sure they can't see us at this window. Get back; I'm about to put the beam on them, to see if they can tell where it's coming from."

"Can they tell?" Royal asked King.

"No, they don't even notice it," King said. "It looks like it's just James and three of his homies there right now. But let's just watch and wait a minute, to make sure and watch every move they make. Let me see, Royal. Move back; I don't want them to see you. Just in case they see us, sit back and relax," King said to Royal.

So, Royal sat back in the corner, while King looked out the window to watch James and his homies' every move.

King watched for about two hours, to make sure it was going to be just James and three of his homies the whole time. All the while, Royal sat in the corner waiting for King say so.

"Okay, Royal, let's go. They've been in the house for about an hour, and it looks like they're not coming out any time soon and that nobody else is coming to his house, either," King said as he started to walk out the room. That was when he noticed he didn't hear any other footsteps but his own. "Royal, Royal," King called out as he walked back in the room. He got to where Royal was and said, "So, this is what we're doing. Royal, get your ass up," King yelled at her as he kicked her foot.

"What, what, aw hey, King," Royal said with sleep in her voice. "Don't aw hey me. How you gonna go to sleep on the job?" King said to Royal.

"My bad, I got bored. Can we go over there now? I'm so bored just sitting here," Royal asked King with complaint in her voice. "Ugh, I can't believe you. Who goes to sleep during a stake out? Royal, that's who," he said as he walked out of the room again. "Royal, let's go," he added with irritation in his voice.

"I'm coming. I'm coming," Royal replied. "Where we going anyways?"

"We going to James' house," King said as they were walking out the back door. "Royal, wait," he whispered. "Because this is a dead end, we can easily get to the house from the back without someone seeing us. All we have to do is keep walking in the back of these houses and around the circle to get to the other side, to get to the back door of James' house."

"Okay, cool," Royal replied.

King and Royal walked through the back, around the circle, to get to James' house.

Chapter Three

"Lean on the right side and I will lean on the left side of house, by the door," King said as he was leaning against the side of the house. "Knock on the door."

"Okay," Royal replied. *Knock, knock*.

"Who is it?" a voice yelled out at the door.

Knock, knock.

"Man, who is it?" the voice yelled out again. Then the door opened and one of James' homies was standing there.

"Man, them damn kids playing again. They play too much. Ughh," James' homie said as he was standing at the end of the back door steps.

"No, it's your girlfriend," Royal said.

"What?" the homie said as he turned around. Then he saw Royal. "Who are you?" he asked Royal.

The next thing she knew, King had

knocked the homie out from behind. "Come on, Royal, stay against the wall and walk leaned over a little, so they won't notice you in the dark," King told her. King and Royal walked down a long, dark hallway for about twenty seconds, then King said, "Shh, wait, hear that, Royal?"

"It sounds like someone is on the phone and coming this way," Royal replied.

"Come on; let's go in this room. Get down behind this table and be quiet," King told Royal.

As they were hiding behind the table, they heard footsteps coming in the room they were in.

"Yeah, I'm home," the voice said to the person he was talking to on his phone.

"It's James," King said, then he crept from behind the table and behind James in the room. "Hang the phone up," he told James, with his gun to his head.

"Okay, okay," James told King as he hung up the phone. "I'll give you whatever you want."

"Empty them pockets," King told him.

"Okay, okay, here is $20,000, my phone and the keys to my car. That's all I got in my pocket," James told King.

"Put it in my bag and walk to the corner with your face against the wall, and don't move until I leave out the door. You hear me?" King ordered.

"Okay, whatever you want," James replied.

As soon as King turned around, *bang*, King fell to the floor. James had shot him.

"Give me my shit back," James said as he grabbed the bag back from King.

Bang. Now, James fell to the floor.

"King, King, oh my God, oh my God, you shot King! Wake up, please," Royal kept saying to her brother as she was shaking him to wake up. Then she heard a gasp for air.

"He shot me; this shit hurts," King said, pain lacing his voice.

"I know, I know. It looks like he just shot you in the left shoulder."

"Raise up; let me see," Royal told King.

"Ugh, Royal, this shit hurts," King said again.

"I know. I'm just trying to see if it went straight through or if it's stuck in the shoulder, or what. It looks like it went straight through," Royal said.

Chapter Four

"What the hell was that, James? James, you okay, homie?" a voice yelled, sounding like it was coming close to where King and Royal were.

"Come on, King, get up. We have to go," Royal said as she grabbed the backpack and helped King up.

King and Royal ran down the dark hallway and out the back door, around the circle behind the houses, to the next block, where King's car was parked.

"Royal, you going to have to drive us to Los Angeles. I can't; I'm in too much pain," King told her.

"What? It's an hour and forty-five minutes long. That's far." "Royal, don't start. We don't have time for all that damn crying right now, so get in the damn car and drive!" King exclaimed in an irritated voice.

"All right, man, fine," Royal replied.

"Give me your phone, so I can turn it off," her brother said as he was turning his own off.

"Here," Royal said as she gave it to him.

"Now, drive," King told his sister.

Royal start driving. For about thirty minutes into the drive, there was silence.

"I'm glad James didn't see you," King said.

"That was James?" Royal asked.

"Yes, I'd know his voice anywhere," King said. "Why, what's wrong? He should be waking up by now."

"What do you mean?" Royal asked.

"What you mean? I mean, you just shot him in his chest, right?" King asked Royal.

Silence followed for a few seconds.

"No, I didn't. Let's just say he won't be waking up," Royal told King as she focused on the road.

"It's okay. You did what you had to do. Don't worry, little sis, this is between us. And I mean between us—we won't even tell Mom and Dad," King told her. "It looks like we're almost there." King and Royal talked for a while, then Royal said, "We're here now. We have to drive down this long driveway, which I don't get why it's that long."

"It's really dark going down this driveway," King commented.

"Finally, we're at the house," Royal said. "I'm going to open the front door while you get out of the car," she told her brother while she opened the door. "Do you need help?"

"No, I'm good," King responded with pain in his voice.

Royal held the door open until King went into the house. "Go sit on the couch until you get your strength to go get cleaned up, so I can clean your wound," Royal said as she closed the door behind herself.

"Okay," King replied.

"So, how long you think we're going to be here before Mom and Dad come?" Royal asked.

"I don't know, maybe a week or so. It just depends on what the news says and what everyone thinks," King answered.

"Oh, well, I'm going to get cleaned up, so I can fix us something to eat, clean and stitch up your wound, and fix your room up so you'll be comfortable," Royal said.

"Okay, I'm just going to lie here for a minute; this gunshot hurts," King said.

"I know. I'm going to clean the wound and stitch you up then give you some pain medication first. Royal walked to the hallway closet to get her mom's medical bag.

"Good," King replied.

Royal got the medical bag out of the closet and walked back to her brother. "Okay. let's take your shirt off so I can clean and stitch it. She helped him take his shirt off, then she started cleaning the wound.

"Ouch, this shot hurts," King said as he jumped a little when Royal started to clean it.

"I know, I know, but you got to be still, so I can clean it properly, Royal told him as she was cleaning his wound. She cleaned and stitched him up, then said, "Now, I'm about to go get cleaned up, and when I get out, I will come and get you so you can clean up.

"Okay," King replied.

Royal went to get cleaned up. When she was finished, she told King, "It's your turn to clean up," as she was walking into the living room.

King was getting up so he could get cleaned up next.

"I'm going to fix your room up while you're in the shower, so when you get out, you'll be able to lie down while I fix us something to eat," Royal told king. "You want some pasta and sauce?" Royal asked.

"Thank you, and yes, I do," he said.

King was in the shower, while Royal fixed up his room. "King, I got your room ready. Now I'm about to fix our food," she yelled through the bathroom door.

"Okay," he yelled back.

Royal went to the kitchen and started cooking. King got dressed and went to his room to rest because his was in so much pain. "King, King," Royal called out as she was walking into his room. "Yeah?" King said with sleep in voice.

"How you feeling?" Royal asked.

"I feel a little better. The pain is going away, but I will need another pain pill after I eat, so I will be able sleep through the night," he told her.

"That's good; let me see it to make sure it's not getting infected and so I can change the bandages," Royal said, "It's not infected yet, so that's good. Now,

I’m about to change the dressing.”

"Is the food ready?" King asked.

"No, in about thirty more minutes," Royal replied as she was charging his bandages. "There, you are all changed now. I’m about to check on the food, and I'll come and get you when it’s ready," she told King. She went back to the kitchen to check on the food, while King lay back down. "It’s time to eat now, King, Royal yelled a little later as she was walking toward his room.

"All right," King said.

"You need help getting up?" Royal asked.

"No, I got it, thank you," King yelled back.

"I’m about to fix your plate, so by the time I get done, you should be in the kitchen, at the table," Royal said, walking back to the kitchen.

"Thank you," King said. "It smells good and everything looks good," he said when he got to the table.

"Thank you, King," Royal said, smiling. "I hope you like it," she added as she was giving him his plate. Royal sat down with her own food and they both start eating. "I hope Daddy and Momma come and get us tomorrow," Royal said after a while.

"Yeah, me too. Well, that was good, sis," King said. "Can you give me another pain pill, so I'll be able to sleep?

"Here you go," Royal said.

Thank you, now get some rest and we'll figure it out tomorrow," King said as he kissed Royal on her forehead.

"Okay," Royal replied with a sigh.

***

The next morning, as she kissed King on the forehead to wake him up, Royal said, "Good morning, King. How you feeling?"

"Good morning," King said as he opened his eyes. "I feel a little better; it doesn't hurt as bad right now."

"That's good. You want some breakfast?"

"Yes, please," he replied.

"What would you like for me to cook?" Royal asked.

"I would like some pancakes and fruit please," her brother said.

"You got it, but let me look at your wound to check it and change your bandages." Royal checked his bandages, "The bleeding has stopped, so that's good. There is no infection, so that's really good. Now, I'm about to clean and change it."

"Hopefully, Mom and Dad come for us soon, or at least tell us what's going on," King said as Royal worked on his bandages.

"Yeah, hope so. There, done," Royal replied. "How many pancakes you want, King?"

Make me three please," King said with a grin.

"Okay, three it is," Royal said.

"Make sure they're fluffy, because you know how you do, trying to make them all thin and shit, like somebody on a diet or something." King looked at Royal and laughed.

"Ha ha, shut up. No, I do not." Royal giggled as she flipped the pancakes over.

"Let me turn on the news and see if there's anything on about what happened last night," King said as he walked to the living room to turn the TV on.

"All right," Royal replied, as King was trying to watch the news. Tell me if you see anything."

"Naw," King replied.

Five minutes went by.

"What about now?" Royal asked again.

"No, girl. Dang, I'm trying to see,"

King replied, irritated.

"All right, fine," Royal said. "The food is ready, so come and get it."

"I'm coming," King said. He sat down and fixed his plate.

"How long you think it will take for Momma and Daddy to find out and come and get us?" Royal asked while sitting down at the table.

"I don't know, but I hope soon, because I need to know what the word is on the streets. I have to figure out what to do next, so our futures can be straight," King said,

"Yes, me too. Well, let's eat first, before the food gets cold, and try to figure stuff out later. I'm hungry, and cold pancakes don't taste good. And they don't do my stomach any good if you know what I mean," Royal said with a laugh.

"You nasty," King replied. Then there was silence between them.

Chapter Five

"King! I got something to tell you," Royal said with nervousness in her tone.

"What's up?" her brother asked with a weird look on his face.

"Well, I saw him shoot you, so I walked up behind him and pulled the trigger," Royal said. There was silence between them for a few seconds.

Then, while he hugged his sister, King said, "Well, you did what you had to do. It's going to be okay, I promise."

"Hopefully, Mom and Dad will be here soon, to get us and help us figure out what to do," Royal said.

"They will, and hopefully, nobody knows about it but us," King said. Just know that whatever happens, I did it. I can't have you locked up because of me. You hear me?" King asked Royal.

"Yes, she said.

"Let's clean the kitchen, and after that, can you check my wound?" he asked.

"Yes, I can," Royal said. They started cleaning the kitchen, and as they were working, she said, "I hope Mom and Dad come before the night is over, because I want to know now."

"Yeah, because I might need to go to the doctor soon. I can't tell if it's bad or not, with these pain pills, and I might need some antibiotics. The pain pills got me out of it," King said. "And I'm not trying to get an infection, either."

"Ha ha, you look a little out of it," Royal said, "but it went straight through so you won't get an infection. You got plenty of pain pills and there are some antibiotics in the cabinet in the bathroom. The kitchen is done, so go into the living room while I go to the bathroom and get the first aid kit. Then I can change your bandage."

"Okay," King said as he walked to the living room.

Royal walked to the bathroom and got the first aid kit, then walked to the living room. "Let me see your shoulder, so I can change your bandages," she said as she sat down on the couch next to him.

King leaned over so she could change his bandages. "Can you make it quick and painless?" he asked, laughing to ease the pain.

"Ha ha, don't tell me what to do, but I'm going to be as gentle as I can be," Royal said. "Again, I wonder how long you think it will take Mom and Dad to find out what happened."

"I don't know, but, like you, I hope soon, because I need to know what's going on too," King replied.

"There, all cleaned up; let's look at the news," Royal said.

"Thank you," King said. "Which channel you think it's on?

"Try the world news, they will probably get it first," Royal suggested.

"True," her brother said as he turned the TV to that channel. Fifteen minutes into watching the news, he commented, "I don't think it's on here; let's see if it's on channel 4.

Right before King was about to change the channel, Royal said, "Look, it just popped up. Don't change it." A few seconds later, she said, "I hope they don't know it was us.

"They won't know or even care," King said.

"Why do you say that?" Royal asked.

"Well, for one, it was an abandoned area, and it was James, the number one drug dealer whom everyone in the city wanted gone, even the crooked cops. They're showing it because it's a crime and someone was murdered. After one or two days, it won't matter anymore because of who it is, and the only one who will care will be his people," King said.

"Yeah, you're right," Royal said, "they're not showing too much."

"I'm about to take a nap," King said.

"Yeah, me too," Royal said as she got up.

"Maybe tomorrow, Mom and Dad will be here," King said as he lay on the couch.

"Yes, maybe," Royal said as she started to walk to her room.

"I'm going to see what's on TV, so I can go to sleep. It's going to be a long few days," king complained to himself. A few minutes later, he said, also to himself, "Damn, there's nothing on TV; I'm just about to go to sleep." Then, a few hours later, he thought to himself, *what's that smell? Whatever it is, it smells good and its coming from the kitchen.* He started walking to the kitchen.

Chapter Six

"Royal! he yelled out.

"Yeah?" Royal replied back.

"You must be cooking, because the house smells like some good food," King said as he walked into the kitchen.

"Yes, I am. I'm cooking your favorites, salmon and salad," Royal said.

"Oh yeah, you knew how to wake me up," he said, chuckling.

" Sit down. You came in just in time. It's done." Royal laughed too, then asked, "How many pieces of salmon you want?"

"Give me three pieces," King replied.

Knowing her brother's appetite, Royal put the salmon on his plate then dished up a healthy serving of salad for him too. Then she asked, "Hey, do want to play some board games after we eat, since we don’t have anything else to do."

"Might as well. We got a lot of time on our hands," King replied. "Okay, cool," Royal said while putting their plates on the table before she sat down.

"Mmm, this looks good, sis," King said just before he dug into his meal.

"Thank you, I fixed it like Momma showed me," Royal said with a smile on her face. "After we get done eating, I’m going to check your wound," she added as they started eating.

"Okay," King said. "And I was right; this is really good, sis."

"Thank you," Royal said, beaming. Several minutes later, she said, "I’m done eating, so let me see your shoulder."

He leaned toward her so she could get a look at the wound. "It looks like there is still no more bleeding so that is good. Let me go get the first aid kit. I'll get that old bandage off, clean the area and put on a fresh dressing," Royal told King.

"By the time you come back and set up everything, I should be done eating," he replied.

"Sounds good," Royal replied as she got up from the table to get the first aid kit from the bathroom. After grabbing the kit, she walked back to the kitchen and said, "Okay, let me see your shoulder without the bandage."

King leaned over towards Royal again. Royal took the bandages off and noted, "It looks good there is still no bleeding, and that should stop by tomorrow. The stitch I put in is holding very well and there is no infection, so that's a good thing too. Now, let me clean it and put on the new bandages."

"That's good, and look at you, doing your doctoring thing," King said.

"Oh, shut up," Royal returned.

"No, but for real, thank you," he said.

"You're welcome," Royal said as she

started cleaning his wound. "When I'm done, can you go find a game for us to play while I'm cleaning the kitchen please?"

"Sure. I hope we have "Sorry"; that's my shit. Can't nobody beat me in that, I'm the champ." King bragged.

"Am I putting your bandages on too tight?" Royal asked king with a laugh.

"No, you good," he said.

"Okay, good. Well, I'm done," Royal said.

"Thanks," King said as he walked to the living room.

"Welcome," Royal replied as she started cleaning the kitchen,

A few minutes went by, and then King yelled out, "Oh, I found it!"

Royal laughed and answered, "Okay, by the time you set everything up, I should be done."

"Sounds good," King yelled back, then he got busy setting up the game.

Just when he sat on the couch and was about to call for Royal, she walked in and sat down on the other side of the couch. "Hey, I brought some chips, dip and your favorite lemonade," she said as she set the snacks on the coffee table next to the game.

"Yes! Now, let's get this butt-whooping started, ha ha," King said.

"Whatever! How about this? Whoever win five games first doesn't have to cook dinner," Royal said.

"Hey," King said, "but it's going to be me, because I'm a master at this game.

"We'll see, Royal said.

Royal and King started playing "Sorry" and one hour had passed, with Royal winning two games and King taking three.

"Well, 'lil sis, it looks like I will be lying back and watching while you be cooking dinner," King said.

"Oh, whatever, you are just up by one," Royal said.

"Well, sorry I win again," King said. "That's luck," Royal said. A few minutes later, she came back with, "*Bam,* I won! I'm three to your four; I'm coming for you." "We'll see about that, because as I'm seeing it, all I need is a six to win, and watch me roll it on this turn," King said as he rolled the dice. King rolled a three. He said, "Oh, man."

"It's my turn, and all I need is a two," Royal said as she rolled. "yes, it's a two. I win again. It's four to four; all I need is one more and I will be the champ and watching you cook." Royal said, laughing.

"Well, big head, that's not going to happen because it's my turn, so just call me the champ," King said as he rolled the dice. A two turned up. "No!" King yelled out in disbelief.

"Yes!" Royal yelled out with excitement. "It's my turn, and I see I need a six. And watch me get it," Royal said as she rolled the dice. The dice rolled a six! "Yes, I win, I win!" Royal yelled out, "I'm the champ, ha ha." Royal ran around the room. "I want chicken and waffles," she said as she stopped running and stood in front of King.

"Whatever, big head, that was luck," King said.

"I'm just glad I don't have to cook. I cooked breakfast and lunch. I'm tired." Royal said with a fake yawn.

"Yeah, yeah, I guess I will cook chicken and waffles," King said as he started to walk to the kitchen.

"While you cook, I will clean this living room up," Royal said while gathering the game pieces.

Chapter Seven

King was in the kitchen cooking and Royal was cleaning the living room when, all of a sudden, there was movement at the front door.

"Oh, shit. Who is that?" Royal whispered to herself.

Then the door opened.

"Royal, baby, thank God, and your brother must be in the kitchen because it smells so good," Royal's mother said.

"Mom, Dad!" Royal said excitedly as she ran up to them and hugged them. "I’m so glad y’all are okay."

"Yes, we're glad you are okay too," Royal and King's parents said.

"Yes, we are," Royal said as she shut the door.

"King, son, what are you cooking that smells so good?" their dad asked.

"Dad!" King exclaimed as he gave him a hug.

"Son," King's mom said as she walked into the kitchen.

"Mom," King said as he let his dad go and went to hug his mother.

"What are you cooking, son?" their mom asked.

"I'm cooking chicken and waffles," King answered, "which will be done in fifteen minutes. Would y'all like some?" King asked. "Yes!" his parents both said at once.

"Okay, cool," King said.

"We'll set the table up for you there," Dad told King.

"Thank you," King said

They set the table while King finished cooking. After a few minutes went by, "The table is ready," their mom said, while she sat down,

"Okay, thank y'all," King said. "The food is done. Royal, can you help put the food on the table?"

"Yes," Royal answered. King and Royal set out the food on the table.

"So, I see y'all had a rough night," their dad said.

"Yes, sir," King and Royal both said as they sat down.

"Tell me what happened," Dad said.

"Okay, so this is what happened," King said, then he told his parents everything.

It was silent in the room for several minutes.

Then their dad asked, "What was the reason again?"

He robbed me, and I was going to go by myself, but as you know, Royal came, even though I told her not to. We were just going to get my stuff back, but it ended up being a self-defense job," King said.

Silence again.

"That's understandable; y'all did what

y'all had to do to protect y'allselves, and y'all are safe. That's all that matters," their dad said.

"So, how is y'all's mentality right now?" their mom asked them. "I'm okay, just taking it one step at a time," King said.

"My mind is everywhere right now, because I don't know what I'm supposed to do," Royal said.

"Don't worry about school, because I called them and told them you had the flu and will be out for a week. I asked them to send your homework. And, King, I called your job and told them you had the flu as well, so don't worry about a note. I got that straightened out," Mom said.

"Thank you," Royal and King both said.

"We came to make sure y'all were all right and to see what happened. We are going back home, to make sure that everything is still the same, which it should be, because he was a wanted man by most everyone in the city, so nobody will care. But we still have to be sure."

"Well, your mother and I are going to leave now. We love y'all and will see y'all soon. Keep the door locked," their dad said as he and their mom walked out of the house.

"We love y'all too, and we will," king said as he was closing the door.

"So, what now?" Royal asked when King turned around from closing the door.

"I don't know; we will have to wait and see," King said.

So, for the next few days, they played games and had cook offs, to pass the time.

At the end of the second day, "I don't think Momma and Daddy coming soon, because they haven't yet," Royal said. As soon as she said it, there was movement at the door.

"Who's at the door?" King asked in a whisper. Then the door opened.

"It’s us, kids," a voice said, coming through the door.

"Mom, Dad, man, I didn’t think y’all ever coming back any time soon," King said.

"Really, son, we were coming," Dad said, laughing.

"I am going to need for everyone to sit here in the living area, so we can talk," Mom said.

"Okay," everyone answered, and they all sat down.

"So, it’s still the same around the city. Nobody knows who did it, and the police don’t care. The investigators are going to make it a cold case, but the only ones who care are his family, which is normal," their mom said. "But how y’all doing and what have y’all been doing?"

"I’m doing okay. I’m just taking it day by day and moving forward," King said.

"Well, I'm okay. I've been having flashbacks of it, but when I have one, I talk to King about it so I can get it out and be able to move past it," Royal said. "We just been playing games and having cook offs to pass the time," she added.

"That's good y'all are finding ways to cope with it and using each other to get through it. I'm proud of y'all," their mom said.

"Me too, and Royal, baby, it's going to get a little hard, but you will get through it because you will have us to help you," their dad added.

"I know, and thank you," Royal said.

"So, what do we do now?" King asked.

"Well, Royal, I called your school and told them it will be another week because you are still sick. So, you will be able to catch up on your homework, and you also have to do a three-page essay, so you will be able to graduate on time next month. Don’t worry; I have a note for you, so you're good on that, but this is the plan for the both of y'all. Royal, a week before you graduate, I need for you to apply to UCT Health Science Center and find housing there, and you are going to keep working at Footlocker until you graduate and become the doctor you want to be. You are going to live your life to the fullest and at peace. And, King, I called your job and told them you need another week, as well, because you are still tired from being sick, and in this week you are home, I want you to apply to every business school you can, so you can get your business license and eventually get your own contracting business and live your life at peace, as well," their mom said to them. "Don't worry. The family think y’all have the flu and I got y’all new phones, so when y’all friends call and ask why it’s been this long to get in touch with y’all, tell them that story. Tell them someone stole y’all phones out the car at the doctor's office. Y'all understand me?" their mother asked.

"Yes, ma'am," Royal and King both answered.

"Okay, good, so your dad and I will be staying the night, and I will be cooking dinner. After dinner, we will clean up and wash everything and get the house back together before we leave out in the morning," Mom said. "Now, Royal, come into the kitchen and help me cook please."

"Yes, ma'am," Royal answered.

"What you going to cook, Momma?" King asked.

Going to cook some curry goat, rice, cabbage, mac and cheese, and cornbread."

"Mmm, we about to eat good," their daddy said.

"Yes, it does sound good, Dad," King said, laughing.

"Come on, Royal," their mom said.

Mom and Royal walked to the kitchen to cook while King and Dad sat in the living room talking among themselves.

Thirty minutes later, "King, Dad, the food will be done in fifteen minutes, but while we're waiting, Momma told me to ask y'all to set up the table please," Royal asked.

"Yes, we can, baby," their dad said, so they all walked to the kitchen, and King and Dad set the table.

A few minutes later, their dad said, "The table is set, my loves," as he sat down.

"Okay, thank you, sweetheart," Mom said. "The food is done."

"It smells good too," King said as he sat down.

"I hope it's good as well," their mom said as she put the food on the table.

"I know it will be," Royal said as she also sat down.

"Now, dig in," their mom said when

everyone was seated.

"You don’t have to tell me but once," King said as he started fixing his plate. Everyone got their food and started to eat and talk.

A few minutes later, their mom asked, "Is everyone done?"

"Yes," they all answered.

"Okay, good. Now, let’s get the house back in order before we go to bed, because we have an early morning," their mom said.

"Okay," everyone agreed and they started to get the house back together, then went to bed.

4:30am came around early.

"King, it’s time to get up. We have to head back to San Diego, so Dad and I can go to work," his mom said.

"All right," King said sleepily.

Then she went to wake Royal, and soon, they were on their way back home. They went back to San Diego, and in the week that Royal and King were home, Royal did all her homework and applied to UTC. King applied to all the business schools he could. When that week was over, Royal went back to school, King went back to work, and as time went on, Royal graduated on time and started at UTC two weeks later. She got an apartment in the area, kept working at Footlocker, and lived her life. She graduated from UTC and became the doctor she always wanted to be, and as for King, he got accepted to DeVry University and graduated at the top of his class. He obtained his business license, got his own contracting business, and lived his life, at peace. It was hard, at times, for them, but they got through it and became successful, at peace with their lives.

The End

About the Author

Joslynn Dixon is a proud Franklin, Tennessee native and a compassionate caregiver in Middle Tennessee. Her passion for helping others shines through both her work and her writing.

As a devoted mother to a lively four-year-old, Joslynn finds joy, purpose, and inspiration in the everyday moments of motherhood, nature and writing.

She enjoys connecting with readers and can be reached on Facebook at Joslynn.Dixon or by email at franklingril@yahoo.com.

More Books by This Author

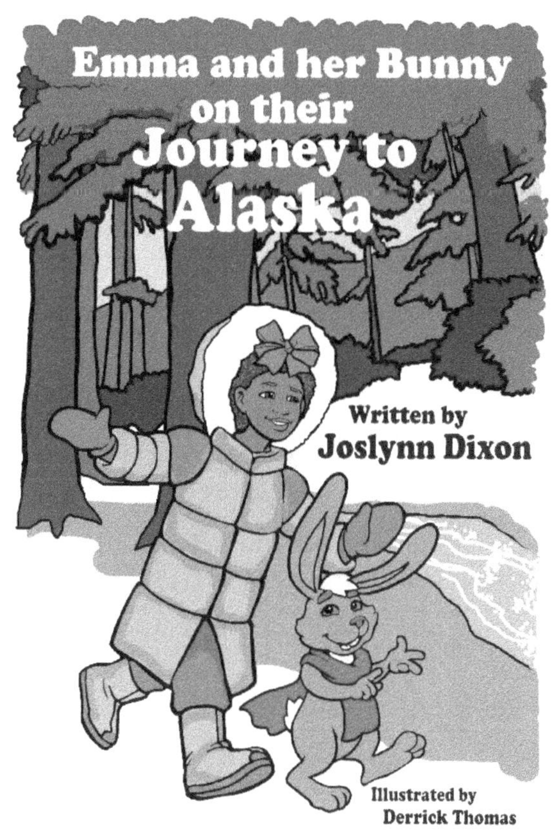
Emma and her Bunny
on their
Journey to
Alaska
Written by
Joslynn Dixon
Illustrated by
Derrick Thomas

www.ingramcontent.com/pod-product-compliance
Lightning Source LLC
LaVergne TN
LVHW010942110826
845149LV00013B/2725
9781955501385